BOOK ANALYSIS

By Elizabeth Smith

Eleanor Oliphant is Completely Fine

BY GAIL HONEYMAN

BrightSummaries.com

BOOK ANALYSIS
Bright Summaries.com
Fifty Shades of Grey Trilogy

GAIL HONEYMAN

SCOTTISH NOVELIST

- **Born in Stirling in 1972.**

Gail Honeyman grew up in Stirling, Scotland. Her mother was a civil servant and her father worked in science. She completed a bachelor's degree in French Language and Literature at Glasgow University, before studying French poetry at postgraduate level at Oxford. She followed her mother into the civil service, then worked as an administrator at Glasgow University. During this job at Glasgow University, Honeyman wrote the first three chapters of *Eleanor Oliphant is Completely Fine* as part of a Faber Academy writing course. Honeyman has mentioned in interviews that another novel is on the way.

ELEANOR OLIPHANT IS COMPLETELY FINE

THE VICTIM OF CHILDHOOD ABUSE STRUGGLES TO MAKE CONNECTIONS AND CONFRONT HER PAST

- **Genre:** novel
- **Reference edition:** Honeyman, G. (2018) *Eleanor Oliphant is Completely Fine.* London: Harper Collins.
- **1st edition:** 2017
- **Themes:** friendship, love, acceptance, mental illness, childhood trauma, loneliness

Gail Honeyman's first novel, *Eleanor Oliphant is Completely Fine*, follows an isolated woman as she tries to mask the impact of childhood trauma through routine, vodka, and a romantic fixation on a musician. Through a series of chance encounters, Eleanor starts to form her first genuine human connections in years, and these new friends help her to process her difficult past. Started as part of a Faber Academy writing course, the novel was extremely well received by critics. Honeyman was awarded the 2017 Costa Debut Novel Award for *Eleanor Oliphant is Completely Fine*, which went on to win the "Debut Book of the Year" award and the "Overall Winner" award (by public vote) in the 2018 British Book Awards.

SUMMARY

CHANCE ENCOUNTERS

Eleanor lives an isolated but highly organised life. She works in an office, calls her mother every week, and drinks two bottles of vodka every weekend. At a concert, she becomes infatuated with a musician called Johnnie Lomond. Her colleagues tease her for being different. She plans to transform her appearance for the musician, starting with a bikini wax. Raymond arrives to fix Eleanor's broken work computer. After work, Eleanor buys a laptop to research Johnnie. Eleanor has a scar on her face. She never knew her father, and her mother told her she was raped. On Wednesday Eleanor talks to her mother, who is in prison, and tells her about Johnnie. Leaving work, Raymond starts a conversation with her. She tries to avoid him, but then an old man collapses in the street and they get him to hospital. Eleanor gets a scheduled visit from a social worker. She has chosen not to find out any more about the traumatic experience that put her in care, but her mother is famous for being "the pretty face of evil" (p. 54). Eleanor has a pot plant called Polly which is the only thing that has survived from her childhood. A document from Eleanor's file has been accidentally left behind by the social worker, reporting Eleanor's difficult behaviour in a foster home. Eleanor was home-schooled after a teacher noticed an injury. It was after a fire that Eleanor's life changed. Eleanor had an abusive first boyfriend called Declan. Eleanor and Raymond visit Sammy, the man who collapsed in the street, in hospital a number of times, and are introduced to his family. Eleanor and Raymond go to the pub after their first visit, and Eleanor walks to the musician's apartment afterwards. On Eleanor's birthday, Raymond invites her to his mum's house. She and Raymond help with the chores. Sammy is being discharged and is going to stay with Laura, who invites them to a party to celebrate. Raymond is attracted to Laura. Eleanor uses a voucher for a free deluxe manicure. After work, she gets a call from her mother, who is angry. Eleanor finds out that Johnnie is appearing at a gig, and decides to go. She has written him a card containing a poem. She goes to a department store after work and buys some new clothes and shoes. She gets a makeover, which conceals her scar. Eleanor eats at McDonald's and heads to the venue, but tickets are sold out. She has a drink at the bar. Eleanor walks to the corner shop the next morning to pick up supplies and vodka, but the shop owner will not sell her alcohol before 10am. She walks to Tesco Extra later to buy vodka, and sees Johnnie there. She tweets him that he should get a Club Card, but he tweets back accusing Tesco of surveillance.

TWO PARTIES AND A FUNERAL

Eleanor and Raymond go together to the party at Laura's house. She offers Eleanor a discount for a haircut. Raymond tells her Laura is gorgeous but not his type. His girlfriend of three years, Helen, has split up with him. Eleanor tells him about her abusive boyfriend, Declan. Raymond calls her a cab and goes back to the party, and Laura. Raymond asks Eleanor to be his plus one to the 40th party of Keith, one of Sammy's sons. She gets a flashy new haircut from Laura. Bob, her boss, offers her a promotion to Office Manager, and she says she will think about it. Eleanor and

Raymond go to a café for lunch, and Eleanor tells Raymond about the promotion offer. At the party, Eleanor does some dancing, but leaves after seeing Raymond dancing with Laura. Eleanor buys some makeup over the weekend and is complemented on her new look by her colleagues. She has decided to accept the promotion. She gets an unexpected Monday call from her mother. Johnnie's tweets reveal that he is leaving his band, Pilgrim Pioneers. In the Wednesday phone call, Eleanor tells her mother about the party and the promotion, and she is scathing about both. Raymond and Eleanor regularly meet for lunch. One day, he passes on the news that Sammy has died. Eleanor buys another new outfit, and Eleanor and Raymond go to Sammy's funeral. At the wake, Eleanor finds Raymond and Laura embracing, and goes off to drink alone at the bar. The bartender tries to take advantage of her drunken state, but Raymond deters him and helps Eleanor to sober up. Later, they go to Raymond's house to drink wine and watch a film. Raymond asks about the scar and Eleanor tells him about the fire when she was 10. She tells him it was started deliberately and that she went into care. Eleanor decides to go to Johnnie's farewell gig with the Pilgrim Pioneers. She books tickets to a different concert so she can scope out the venue, and invites Raymond, but accidentally chooses a "grindcore" (p. 252) concert, which she finds horrifying.

'BAD DAYS'

Eleanor drinks multiple bottles of vodka and has laid out painkillers, drain cleaner, and a knife, in preparation to kill herself. Polly the plant has died. At the concert, she had realised that Johnnie did not see her, would not be attracted to her, and was not the person she thought he was. A smoke machine had also given her flashbacks. Eleanor goes out to buy more vodka. Raymond finds her after she was missed at work. He cleans the house, makes her soup, buys her flowers, and looks after her. Eleanor at first rejects Raymond's suggestion that she might have a mental illness, but eventually agrees to go to the doctor. She is diagnosed with depression, given time off work, and referred to a therapist, Maria Temple. She refuses medication. She goes and buys herself a vodka to cope after her first session. She continues to meet Raymond regularly for lunch. She tells him her mother is in prison, but she cannot remember why. She was given a new identity. Raymond offers to find out about her past, but she declines. Eleanor's mother orders her not to talk about her childhood. Eleanor meets Laura, who tells her she has been seeing Raymond. At the next session, Maria asks about Eleanor's lack of a father figure, and her mother's controlling attitude. In care, only her physical needs were met, not her emotional ones. Eleanor starts to remember somebody – a child from her flashbacks. Eleanor snaps at Maria, but Maria says anger is a good sign. Eleanor decides to tidy up her apartment. She is given flowers by her colleagues at the office. Raymond brings her a black cat with bald patches from when it was put in a burning dustbin. Raymond later brings his mother to see her, and buys her cake. Raymond leaves behind a newspaper with an article about the recent success of Pilgrim Pioneers, without Johnnie.

FACING THE PAST

At a session with Maria, Eleanor visualises the fire, remembering her mother's anger at her, and the other child, Marianne. Eleanor meets

Raymond for lunch on Sunday. Raymond is hungover, having seen Laura the night before. He says he will not be seeing her again, as they do not have much in common. Raymond confesses he has been researching Eleanor's mother. He asks Eleanor if she wants to read any of the articles, but she says she can find out herself when she is ready. Eleanor tells Maria that Marianne was her little sister. She has been blocking out the painful memories. Later, Keith, Sammy's son, gives her Sammy's red sweater. On the bus on the way to therapy, Eleanor notices that people avoid sitting next to her. She starts to panic, and a kind stranger asks if she is alright. She realises she sometimes judges people unnecessarily, because of her mother. One night her memories come back. In the following counselling session, Eleanor finally admits that "Mummy's a bad person" (p. 350). She is terrified that she has inherited this badness, and decides to break off contact with her. Her mother set the fire to kill her children, but only Marianne died. Eleanor has survivor's guilt and feels she should have protected her little sister. Eleanor and Raymond go for coffee after the session. She tells him about her mother starting the fire and asks Raymond for help finding out about her past. Eleanor goes back to work. She is anxious, but Raymond supports her. She offers to organise the Christmas lunch, and is given flowers and well-wishes by her colleagues. Raymond has sent her a message asking her to a classical music concert. Eleanor confronts her mother and says goodbye. She asks Raymond to sit with her in their café as she reads two articles that reveal that not only Marianne died, but also their mother, Sharon Smyth. Eleanor tried to re-enter the house to rescue her sister, who was in a wardrobe. Eleanor realises she has been pretending her mother is still alive. She has decided to request her social services file and read it. Raymond and Eleanor arrange to go to the concert.

CHARACTER STUDY

ELEANOR OLIPHANT

Eleanor works in an office, sorting accounts for a graphic design firm. She does the crossword daily and enjoys solving problems, but cannot "solve the problem of [her]self" (p. 267). At a concert, she becomes infatuated with a musician called Johnnie Lomond, believing that this relationship will solve her problems, make her normal, and meet her mother's strict standards. She thinks of her appearance as "matte, dull and scuffed" (p. 166), which leads to an attempt to improve herself on the outside for the benefit of Johnnie. She has a scar on her face as a result of a fire when she was 10 years old, which acts as a constant reminder of her traumatic past. In her mission to impress Johnnie, she struggles comically with the conventions of society. She often fails to re-cognise herself as the source of awkwardness in social encounters, instead blaming the "under-developed social skills" (p. 50) of the people she interacts with. Eleanor's obsessively organised routine is a coping mechanism, designed to numb her feelings. The two bottles of vodka she drinks to get through each weekend also help to numb her to life, and to suppress her memories of the fire and her childhood abuse. Eleanor has internalised the abusive language of her mother, who calls her weekly and tells her she is "a pointless waste of human tissue" (p. 212). It is gradually revealed that her mother is responsible for the fire that burned Eleanor and killed her sister, and, in a final twist, that she was also killed and Eleanor has been imagining their conversations. Eleanor has also been suppressing memories of her younger sister, Marianne, whom she adored. She blames herself for Marianne's death, and has held herself incapable of caring for anyone since. After the fire, Eleanor was given a new name and put into the care system, where she was starved of affection. Although she was academically bright and gained a good degree in classics at university, she was sexually and physically abused by her first and only boyfriend, Declan. She learned to function on her own, and to put up emotional defences, but this has contributed to her extreme loneliness. However, Sammy's accident forces Eleanor to forge a number of new friendships, and she finds the genuine human warmth she has been missing. She becomes particularly close to Raymond, despite initially disapproving of his slovenly appearance. Due to disillusionment over the musician, she has a breakdown and tries to kill herself. With the help of Raymond, and a therapist called Maria, Eleanor is able to process the trauma in her past and to start to accept herself.

'MUMMY'

Sharon Smyth, "the pretty face of evil" (p. 54), abused her two daughters, taking them out of school when their teacher noticed bruises. Finally, she set fire to the house and made sure the girls could not escape. She died herself in the blaze, and Eleanor, her eldest, escaped. When Eleanor asked about her father, her mother told her she was raped. After her death, Eleanor fabricates a relationship with her mother because she feels she is all she has left. 'Mummy' is also an externalisation of Eleanor's own negative self-talk, which is in itself a result of her childhood abuse. Her mother becomes the voice telling her that she is worthless, whilst also judging others to an impossible standard. Eleanor's fixation on Johnnie results in part from her need to appease this voice. Eleanor still craves her mother's approval, despite being crippled by her abuse – towards the end of the novel, she admits: "I wanted Mummy to love me" (p. 267). At the same time, she is terrified that she will have inherited something evil from her. A turning point comes when Eleanor learns to identify the harmful nature of 'Mummy' and to cut off contact from her, finally admitting that she was never there at all.

JOHNNIE LOMOND

As the musician Eleanor becomes obsessed with, Johnnie's role in the novel is mostly comedic. He is a stereotypically arrogant musician, and most of his comic value comes from the disjunction between who Eleanor thinks he is, and the evidence the reader is given. Although he dresses well, Johnnie is self-obsessed and lacks self-awareness. He mistreats his fellow band members until they force him out of the group. Immediately after this, they become very successful without him, to Johnnie's horror. Eleanor's idea of Johnnie is a projection of her mother's standards, and bears little resemblance to his actual character, and Eleanor is devastated when she realises this.

BOB

To begin with, Eleanor views her boss, Bob, as somewhat tired and incompetent. However, he becomes a more sympathetic character as Eleanor interacts more with him. He organises flowers for Eleanor and is understanding about her depression because his sister also suffers from it.

RAYMOND GIBBONS

Raymond recently started at the IT department of Eleanor's workplace. He was the first person in his family to go to university, but his father died before he could complete his degree, and he is still coming to terms with this loss. He is devoted to his mother, who is kind and loving. Raymond has a healthier social life than Eleanor, although his girlfriend of three years, Helen, recently split up with him. He is initially attracted to Laura, but eventually realises they do not have enough in common. At first, he does not fit any of Eleanor's standards for being a decent man. She finds him scruffy, "adolescent" (p. 99) and a bit flabby, and objects to his "grubby hooded sweatshirt and dirty training shoes" (p. 97). For his part, Raymond finds her "a right nutter" (p. 359) to start with. However, as they spend more time together, they form a strong bond. Raymond shows her the kind of genuine interest and friendship she has not known since Marianne. He helps Eleanor through her hardest times and possibly saves her life, even bringing her a cat to help her cope.

MRS GIBBONS

Raymond's mother, Mrs Gibbons, represents everything Eleanor never had. She is the archetypal "mother, a kind, loving woman" (p. 112), to such an extent that these qualities completely define her. She is immediately kind and accepting of Eleanor, who helps her to feel a little less lonely herself. She is extremely proud of her son, Raymond.

SAMMY THOM

Sammy is an old man in a red jumper who collapses, causing Eleanor and Raymond to call him an ambulance. As he recovers in hospital, he treats Eleanor and Raymond as part of his large, loving family. He is very warm and generous, and insists on living life to the fullest, through drinking, smoking, spending time with his family, and wearing an outrageous red jumper. Eleanor admires the unconventionality of the jumper and the attitude it seems to represent. After bringing the characters together, Sammy dies and is mourned and missed by all. Eleanor is later given the red jumper by his son Keith.

LAURA

Laura is Sammy's youngest daughter She is a hairdresser and, unlike his other two children, who are in stable relationships, she has been divorced twice. She is very attractive and glamorous, and shares some of this glamour with Eleanor, who thanks her for "making [me] shiny" (p. 177). At first, Raymond is attracted to her, and she is attracted to Raymond for his stable, caring personality. She is at times jealous of Eleanor and Raymond's closeness, and Eleanor responds with similar feelings. However, Raymond recognises that she is "high maintenance" (p. 333) and that they do not have much in common, so he breaks it off, realising that he would be better suited to someone more genuine.

MARIA TEMPLE

Maria is Eleanor's new therapist, who she is referred to by her GP after her breakdown. In their first session, Eleanor is horrified when she realises that Maria is "fun" (p. 287). However, as their meetings go on, Maria helps Eleanor to access the traumatic memories and feelings that she has been suppressing. She is patient, professional, and good at her job.

MARIANNE

Marianne is Eleanor's little sister, who tragically died in the fire. Eleanor was a caring and protective older sister, later blaming herself for her death. Eleanor tells Maria that she "failed her" (p. 353) and feels guilty for surviving, even though a newspaper article later reveals that Eleanor tried to rescue her from the flames. Marianne is the reason Eleanor does not think herself capable of looking after anyone or anything, so she cuts herself off. Eleanor has been suppressing the memory of Marianne, which comes out in unsettling dreams. It takes therapy and self-acceptance to come to terms with the truth.

ANALYSIS

TRAUMA AND MENTAL ILLNESS

At the start of the novel, Eleanor deals with her traumatic past by numbing her flashbacks and feelings with vodka and a mindless routine. She lives in denial, pretending she does not have emotional needs and that she is "fine, fine, fine" (p. 160). However, these methods fail to prevent her flashbacks from the fire. After her project with the musician fails, she has a depressive episode, realising that "I was Eleanor, sad little Eleanor Oliphant, with my pathetic job, and my vodka and my dinners for one, and I always would be" (p. 264). Her fixation with Johnnie was an attempt to find completeness while appeasing the internalised voice of her mother. The reader is directly exposed to the negative patterns Eleanor falls into, and the low self-esteem caused by her abusive mother, even if Eleanor cannot at first recognise these things herself. Even after her suicide attempt, she denies being mentally ill, but eventually Raymond coaxes her into going to her GP. After being diagnosed with depression, she is able to accept that she is not "fine" (p. 160) after all. Paradoxically, this recognition allows her to process her trauma and slowly become genuinely "in all the ways that matter... fine" (p. 381). Honeyman uses first person narration to allow the reader to witness the crippling effects of childhood trauma and mental illness first hand. The reader can therefore empathise not just with the fictional Eleanor, but also with those who suffer from mental illnesses or fail to fit in outside the novel. The elements of humour in the novel also serve to humanise the sufferers of mental illness: Eleanor is not just another victim.

LONELINESS

As a result of feeling that she does not fit in, and avoiding connection, Eleanor suffers from extreme loneliness. She struggles with feelings of worthlessness, and only the small act of watering and talking to her pot plant reassures her that she is not "a figment of [her] own imagination" (p. 5). As painful as Eleanor's loneliness is, she feels on some level that "it was no more than [she] deserved" (p. 160), still blaming herself for the death of her sister, the only other person she was close to. Through Eleanor, Honeyman comments that loneliness is "the new cancer – a shameful, embarrassing thing, brought upon yourself in some obscure way" (p. 270). The novel therefore serves to break this taboo, and to shed some light on a surprisingly common issue in society today. There is a similar stigma surrounding mental health. In fact, even the title of the novel highlights the fact that "If someone asks how you are, you are meant to say FINE" (*ibid.*), even if you are not.

FRIENDSHIP

Eleanor avoids human connection because she thinks she is not worthy of it, and will only let down the people she loves. This attitude is a result of her childhood trauma and losing her sister, the only person to love her unconditionally. In care, she was only able to form temporary attachments, and acknowledging her pain only led to being "moved somewhere else" (p. 281) by foster carers who were not prepared to address her problems. After an abusive relationship with Declan, her first and only boyfriend, Eleanor put up further emotional barriers. However, these barriers are gradually eroded by the warmth of characters like Sammy, Mrs Gibbons, and Raymond. Raymond's friendship helps Eleanor through her breakdown, and with his support she is able to take steps like starting therapy and returning to work. Eleanor thinks of herself as unworthy of friendship, and is surprised that Raymond does not lose interest after he sees her in an emotionally vulnerable state. Just as Raymond accepts Eleanor even at her worst, she learns to look past his scruffiness, and therefore to shed the internalised judgement of her mother's voice. Ultimately, his friendship gives her hope for the future, and helps her to open up to the world, even if that involves becoming emotionally vulnerable. Realising the impact of this friendship on her, Eleanor feels "the gentle heat of something opening, the way some flowers spread out in the morning at the sight of the sun" on "the unscarred piece of [her] heart" (p. 358).

FITTING IN

Eleanor's failure to correctly judge or participate in social conventions reveals how bizarre some of these conventions are. Her initial goal of "successful camouflage as a human woman" (p. 30) is humorously difficult to obtain, considering Eleanor is already a "human woman". By manipulating her appearance in ways that the novel exposes as illogical and arbitrary, Eleanor makes herself more "acceptable" (p. 230) to her colleagues and acquaintances. The friendliness of her colleagues seems particularly conditional on the conformity of her appearance. Through Eleanor's adventures in beauty and grooming, Honeyman exposes the absurdity of social rituals and unrealistic beauty standards. However, Eleanor's makeover does signal increased participation in the world, which she was previously numb to. Eleanor herself acknowledges that "social success is often built on pretending just a little" (p. 237), but, partly due to her trauma, she approaches life by being "truthful with the world" (*ibid.*). This approach contributes to her position as an outsider, but it also provides an illuminating perspective on society. In the end, just as Eleanor admired Sammy for living life to the fullest, as a pensioner in a bright red jumper, Raymond admires Eleanor for refusing to pretend. Fitting in at first appears to be a matter of looking a certain way and participating in certain social rituals. However, as the novel goes on, it is Eleanor's most meaningful social connections that bring her a sense of belonging, and these are not necessarily predicated on "pretending" (*ibid.*). In fact, her relationship with Raymond is based on mutual honesty and vulnerability, and Raymond respects and admires the qualities that made her partially an outsider. Honeyman reveals that all Eleanor needed to find her "Eleanor-shaped social hole" (*ibid.*) was friendship and acceptance.

FURTHER REFLECTION

SOME QUESTIONS TO THINK ABOUT…

- Why do you think Eleanor chose Johnnie to fixate on, rather than somebody nearer to hand?
- In the last chapters of the book, Raymond and Eleanor become even closer, and Raymond asks Eleanor to go to a concert with him, appearing tentative afterwards. Given the nature of their bond, and the fact that Laura was at one point jealous of Eleanor, do you think that Raymond and Eleanor could become romantically involved? Or will they remain friends? Why do you think Honeyman chose to leave this ambiguous?
- What role do you think Laura has in the novel? Does she represent an unattainable standard for Eleanor, or prove that that standard does not necessarily lead to happiness? Explain your answer.
- Why do you think Eleanor was so fond of Sammy's red jumper?

- Based on the novel, do you think it is possible to control the influence of the past? Can difficult memories be addressed without allowing them to overwhelm the present?
- Given that Eleanor has internalised her mother's negative opinions since childhood, is it possible to completely separate her mother's voice from her own internal dialogue? If not, is this necessarily a bad thing?
- At the start of the novel, Eleanor decides to transform herself from the outside in, changing her appearance and hoping that her feelings will follow. Do you think this is a sustainable approach? Could the opposite method, from the inside out, be more successful?
- Why do you think Eleanor imagined conversations with her mother rather than Marianne, given that both of them died in the fire? Think about guilt and self-punishment.

We want to hear from you!
Leave a comment on your online library
and share your favourite books on social media!

FURTHER READING

REFERENCE EDITION

- Honeyman, G. (2018) *Eleanor Oliphant is Completely Fine*. London: Harper Collins.

www.brightsummaries.com

Ebook EAN: 9782808019668

Paperback EAN: 9782808019675

Legal Deposit: D/2019/12603/150

Cover: © Primento

Digital conception by Primento, the digital partner of publishers.